GW00480484

To _____

*From* _____

*With Love*
*xxx*

### *Beryl Matthews*

From tea girl to singer to credit controller, Beryl Matthews has enjoyed a variety of careers but her interest in writing has remained constant. She grew up in a family of avid readers and books have always been an important part of her life. Beryl Matthews lives in Hampshire with her husband. She is the author of two Barley Books Handbag Romances.

*Beryl Matthews*

# Links of Love

Published by Barley Books Ltd 2001.

ISBN: 1902691113

Printed  and bound in Great Britain by. Cox &
Wyman Ltd, Cardiff Road, Reading, Berkshire.

Barley Books
PO Box 103
Leeds
West Yorks
LS16 9YD.

# LINKS OF LOVE

Another ball veered off to the left and Kate Palmer watched it with resignation. She wished she had the courage to tell her client that he was wasting his money and would never make a golfer. The temptation was great but she couldn't dash his hopes of spending his retirement on the golf course, so rather than advising him to take up fishing instead, she prised the club from his fingers and gave a tight smile.

'Let me show you again, Mr Robertson.' She placed the ball on the tee, stopped him in mid-swing, took her stance - all the time explaining what she was doing and why - then hit the shot straight down the middle of the practice ground.

He scowled but she ignored it, wound his fingers around the club and pushed him into the proper address position. 'Now stay exactly like that and take the club back smoothly.'

He started the action.

'No!' She stopped him in mid-swing. 'You have shifted your grip and moved your feet.'

'I haven't!' he exclaimed indignantly. He'd gone red in the face with anger and frustration now, and she longed to walk away, but this was her job. A job she needed. But after very little sleep last night, her patience was at an end.

'Very well,' she said as calmly as possible, 'hit the ball like that.'

It sailed off in a vicious hook, left the practice ground, hit a tree and bounced across the terrace outside the clubhouse where members were enjoying a drink in the sun. She shaded her eyes, checking to see if it had found a human target, but it didn't look as if it had and she breathed a sigh of relief.

'You really meant that, didn't you?' she remarked dryly. 'I don't think anyone has ever reached there before.'

'It's your fault!' The club landed with a thud at her feet. 'You couldn't teach a child to play tiddlywinks. I can't understand a prestigious club like this employing a woman professional. Just because your name's Palmer doesn't mean you know the first damned thing about golf. And you look as if you've been up all night - clubbing somewhere, I suppose,' he said in disgust. 'I'm going to lodge a complaint.'

She watched him storm away and with a sigh bent to pick up the club. When she turned to put it back into the bag, her attention was caught by a man standing a few feet away watching her intently. He was well over six feet; thirty-something, she guessed, black hair and blue eyes, and he looked completely out of place on a golf course. He was wearing a dark grey suit, a pristine white shirt and a blue silk tie almost the same colour as his eyes.

Kate hoisted the bag of clubs onto her shoulder and was about to ask if he needed any help when he spun on his heel and marched towards the clubhouse. It must be my day for meeting rude men, she concluded with a grimace.

She wandered back to the shop deep in thought. She liked her job, but times like this made her sad, as this wasn't the kind of life she'd mapped out for herself. At the age of nineteen she had earned her Players' Card and had started competing on the professional circuit with such hope and delight. In her first tournament she had come fifteenth, the second one she was sixth, and after two days of the third she had been in the lead by two strokes. Then

the dreadful news had arrived and that
had been the end of her dreams.

Had it really been five years ago?

'You're wanted upstairs,' Dave, her
assistant told her as soon as she walked
through the door. 'The boss himself.'

'That was quick.'

'You know Mr Robertson,' he said,
shaking his head. 'That man's never
going to be fit enough to enjoy his
retirement if he doesn't calm down.'

'I know, but how do you tell
someone that he will never be able to
play golf, even if he was taught by Nick
Faldo himself?' She sat down to
change her shoes. 'The problem is he
doesn't like me; in fact I don't think he
likes any women. I wish you'd take him
for his lessons, Dave, he might listen to
a man.'

A look of horror crossed his face.
'Not likely! Anyway, he wouldn't want
me; I'm only the assistant Pro. The
man's rolling in money, so I've been

told, and he wouldn't waste his time on someone as lowly as me.'

Kate thought that judgement was a bit harsh, but she didn't make any comment as she ran a comb through her short pale blonde hair and applied a touch of lipstick, ignoring the dark smudges under her green eyes. 'Do I look tidy enough?'

'Beautiful as ever.' He regarded her affectionately. 'Have a cup of tea before you enter the lion's den.' Dave reached for the kettle.

'No, better get it over with.'

'Don't look so worried,' he told her, 'Gordon knows how talented you are. He won't listen to Mr Robertson.'

It was hard to smile but she managed it. There was a nasty feeling in the pit of her stomach about this, and for some reason she couldn't fathom she couldn't rid her mind of that man with the piercing blue eyes. What had he been doing watching her like that and why did he have such a profound effect upon her?

'Dave?'

'Hmm?'

'Have you seen a tall man dressed in a smart business suit around here?'

He shook his head. 'No, all I've seen are the usual crowd of golfers. Why?'

'Oh, he was out on the practice field, that's all.'

Her assistant laughed. 'He must have stuck out like a sore thumb dressed like that.'

'He did.'

'I expect he's meeting someone.'

'Yes, probably.' She headed for the door. 'Wish me luck.'


'You can go in now, Miss Palmer.' The secretary held open the door for her.

Taking a deep breath, she walked into the office and the first thing she saw was a smug-looking Mr Robertson. Her unease deepened. That look told her all she needed to know; he was flushed with success.

'Ah, Kate.' Gordon Hersey didn't smile. 'You know what this is about?'

Of course she did. She'd been well aware that Mr Robertson had it in for her from the minute he'd joined the club. She just couldn't understand why. She had always been polite and professional with him - except today when she had allowed him to hit that shot, knowing full well that it was going to sail out of the practice ground.

She dredged up a smile and lied. 'I really can't imagine.'

'I've received a serious complaint about you.'

Suddenly she was weary of everything. Weary of trying to be on top form when she was dropping with fatigue; weary of the worry.

'Kate?'

Gordon's voice cut through her sombre thoughts. 'What am I supposed to have done?'

'You've been rude and unprofessional,' Mr Robertson butted in. 'I've paid good money for lessons and you've acted as though it has been too much trouble for you. You've never had the slightest interest in teaching me and I haven't had value for my money.'

'That's not true!' His accusations stung. She had always given one hundred and ten percent in an effort to teach him how to strike a ball correctly, but it was useless. Some people just didn't have an eye for a ball and no amount of lessons could change that. Holding his gaze, she said as calmly as possible, 'If you are dissatisfied with the instruction you've received, I'll be happy to refund you for the lessons.'

He gave a humourless laugh. 'And you think that will make it all right, do you?'

'No, but I'm prepared to do that, even though I disagree with your opinion about my attitude.'

Gordon cleared his throat, his glance sliding past her, then coming back to settle on her face again. 'If it isn't true, then why has Mr Robertson brought this to my attention?'

'I really don't know. I've done my best, Gordon, but learning to play golf takes patience and hours of practice.'

'I've got plenty of patience,' the man exploded. 'You're the one who's no good.' He turned to Gordon. 'Get rid of her and employ a *proper* Professional.'

Kate's head shot up. Who was he to give Gordon orders? There was more to this than a complaint about her conduct.

'Have you been having a difficult time, Kate?' Gordon asked, looking decidedly uncomfortable.

'No more than usual, and I have *never* let it interfere with my job, you know that.'

He cast another quick glance to the back of the room. 'Nevertheless, I can't ignore this. Your contract runs out at the end of the month, and under the circumstances, we don't feel we can renew it.'

The news hit her like a physical blow but she managed to keep her voice steady. 'I have worked here for five years, and in all that time there has never been a complaint against me. Does that count for nothing?'

'I'm sorry.'

That brief sentence sealed her fate; she was numb and so damned tired. 'I'll be out by the end of the month.'

Turning carefully in case her legs let her down and she disgraced herself, she faced the door. Then she saw him. He was leaning against the wall, and she realised that he'd been there all the time, a silent witness to her humiliation. So that's who Gordon had been looking at. Who was he, and was her dismissal down to him? After all, he had been watching them on the practice ground, so had he misinterpreted things and backed up Mr Robertson?

Anger surged through her, bringing her back to life. 'Is this your doing?' she demanded.

He pushed himself away from the wall and strode towards her, and although his movements were fluid and relaxed, there was no doubt about the sharp intelligence reflected in his brilliant eyes.

Mr Challoner has nothing to do with this.' Gordon spoke sharply.

'You've had a wasted journey.' Mr Robertson was triumphant.

'So it would seem.' The deep tone of his voice gave nothing away.

Kate glanced from man to man, puzzled by this charged exchange, then she looked up at Mr Challoner. 'What's this all about?'

He didn't have to answer because

suddenly it all became clear. She'd
heard rumours but hadn't taken any
notice of them. She grimaced in disgust.
'Money!'

The slight inclination of Mr
Challoner's head told her that her guess
was correct. With a last fulminating
glance at everyone present, she left.

'What's the matter, Kate, had a bad
day?' Her father handed her a cup of
tea.

'Terrible! I've lost my job.' Her
voice wobbled, and as her father
inhaled sharply, she pulled herself
together. Self-pity was not going to help
their situation. 'I'm all right until the
end of the month, and I'll soon get
something else,' she added hastily,
trying to sound positive. 'Surrey is
crowded with golf courses.'

'What happened?'

She told him the story and watched
the colour drain from his lined face. He

was old before his time, she thought sadly. 'I'll put an ad in the paper and see if I can get some private clients. I'm a good teacher, no matter what Mr Robertson says.'

'I know you are.' He squeezed her hand reassuringly. 'Who do you think this other man was?'

'I haven't got a clue, but I don't think Mr Robertson liked him.'

Her father laughed. 'Does he like anyone?'

She shrugged. 'He might be wealthy, but he isn't a happy man. It was cruel of him to get me dismissed like that, I don't even know if I'll be able to get a reference.'

'I agree, but I don't want you worrying about it. We'll get through, and while you're looking for another post, I might be able to get some overtime.'

'Oh, you mustn't,' she protested. 'You are already doing too much.'

'And you're not?' His smile was sad.

'Kate! That you?' a voice called from the other room.

She was immediately on her feet. 'Coming Paul.' She turned to her father and kissed his cheek. 'You'd better be off.'

'OK, sweetheart. He hasn't been too bad today.'

'Good.' She pinned a smile on her face and hurried to her brother.

'Hallo, Sis.' Paul beamed. 'Had a good day?'

'Smashing!' She would never let him know if she was unhappy because he had enough to deal with. 'What would you like for dinner?'

'I fancy pasta with one of your lovely garlicky sauces.'

'Then that's what you shall have.' She pushed his chair into the kitchen so he could watch her work.

'You look tired, Kate. I'm sorry I kept you awake so much last night.'

'I'm fine, don't you worry about it.'

'But I do!' His eyes clouded with concern. 'This isn't right. You and Dad have given up everything to look after me.'

'We are happy to do it, Paul. You know that.'

He nodded, then looked down at his helpless hands. 'If only I could move my arms, then I'd be able to do more for myself.'

She left the peppers she was chopping for the sauce and knelt in front of him. 'You will be able to, Paul. The doctors have all said that you could regain some movement in time, even walk again.'

'I know.' He sighed. 'But it's been five years and you've spent a fortune trying to find a cure for me.'

'And we'll keep on,' she told him confidently, and then went back to her preparations for dinner. 'You'll get through this, Paul. I'm confident that you *will* be able to walk again one day.'

'Yes, mustn't give up hope.'

She couldn't help wondering if he had given up, and if that was the reason he wasn't recovering as he should be.

'Can we surf the Net tonight?' he asked, his gloomy look disappearing.

'All right, but nothing medical.'

'OK. Dad's bought me a new golf program. We can try that out, as well.'

Once dinner was out of the way, they went to the computer and Paul watched avidly as she searched for the websites he wanted, then she loaded the game into the computer. The next hour was boisterous and Paul won easily.

He grinned hopefully at her. 'As soon as I'm on my feet again, I'll challenge you to a proper round of golf.'

'You'll have to give me a five shot handicap then.' She joined in his fun. 'You always were better than me.'

'What? I'll give you two.'

'You're on!'

The news had spread and the next day the shop was continually full of members. The request for lessons grew until she hardly had a space left. She was touched by everyone's kindness.

At lunchtime the club Captain stormed into the shop. 'Kate, I've just been told that you've been dismissed. It's scandalous, you're the best Pro we've ever had, and I've told this stupid management team that.'

She smiled. 'Thank you, James, but you're wasting your time. Do you know what's going on?'

'Well, I can't get a straight answer out of Gordon, but I've been speaking to a friend of mine who usually knows everything that's going on in the leisure industry.' He sat down. 'Any chance of a cup of tea?'

'Coming right up.'

James didn't speak while he was waiting for his tea and Kate worked quickly, anxious to hear what he'd discovered.

'What did your friend say?' she prompted, handing him the mug.

'It seems that the owners are in financial difficulties and there's speculation about a hostile bid being launched.'

Dave whistled through his teeth and joined them. 'So that's what this is all about.'

'But what is it to do with my contract not being renewed?'

'Ah, well, that's the nasty bit.' James took a gulp of tea. 'If my information is correct, Robertson is one of this company's main backers and he's probably just given them more money.'

Kate shook her head. 'I still don't understand.'

'He's got a nephew and part of the deal is that he be given your job. He doesn't like women in a golf club, and has objected to you being employed as the Pro from the moment he joined because of the simple fact that you're female.'

'I didn't stand a chance then, did I?'

James shook his head. 'No, and we're all so disgusted about it that we are thinking of leaving and joining another club.'

'Oh, don't do that,' she urged. 'Chiverton Oaks is a beautiful course and you'd be hard pressed to find its equal.'

'We know.'

Dave stirred another spoonful of sugar in his tea. 'Do you know anything else about this hostile bid?'

'Not much, but rumour has it that someone wants to turn this into a country club. You know that spare ground they were thinking of making into a nine-hole course?'

They nodded.

'Well, it's a perfect site for an hotel with a swimming pool, gym, and full leisure facilities.'

'If it's true then I can understand the owners being worried.' Kate grimaced. 'Serves them right for issuing shares. It's made them vulnerable to market influences.

'Yes. Quite a few investors have already sold out, that's how we know about it.'

James looked at her kindly. 'What you going to do, Kate?'

'I'll soon find something else.' She smiled brightly to disguise her concern.

'Of course you will.' Dave squeezed her shoulder. 'You're the best; someone will snap you up.'

'How's Paul?' James asked.

'About the same.'

'No sign of improvement, then?'

'No, but we keep on hoping. The doctors can't understand it, he should have started regaining some movement a long time ago, but something is holding him back.'

'Pity the police never caught that hit

and run driver; you might have been able to get compensation then. Is the case still open?'

'No. Unless some new evidence comes to light, they can't do any more. The driver got out of his car and stood looking at Paul, then left him and drove away. My brother was able to give the police a description of him, though I don't know how good it was because they've never managed to track him down, but he insists that he'd know him if he ever saw him again.'

'Callous beast,' James exploded. 'People like that should be charged with attempted murder or something.'

'Paul saw the car and is certain it was a Jag, but he was in too much pain to read the number plate, and he lost consciousness as it drove away.'

'James.' The club secretary looked through the door. 'Don't forget we've got a meeting in ten minutes.'

'I'm coming.' He stood up. 'You

take care now, Kate, and don't leave without saying goodbye.'

Her last day at the club arrived all too soon and she was sad to leave everyone. In the five years she had worked at this lovely course, she had made many friends, and now she would have to start all over again. That was if she could get another job. The worry was like a physical ache.

'I don't know how we're going to manage,' Dave complained. 'You're leaving today and there's no sign of anyone taking your place.'

'No, that's odd. I would have expected him to have arrived days ago.' She gave a humourless laugh. 'I expect he will turn up as soon as I drive away.'

'Yeah, if it is Robertson's nephew, he's probably ashamed to show his face.'

At that moment the door swung open and Mr Challoner strode in, only this time he wasn't dressed for the office, he was wearing black jeans and a black knit shirt. Kate's breath caught in her throat. For such a big man he moved with surprising, almost feline, grace, and he was impressive whatever he was wearing.

'Are you the new Professional?' Dave asked, before he'd hardly stepped inside the shop.

He shook his head. 'I don't know the first thing about the game.' Then he walked over to Kate and handed her a card. 'Go and see this man tomorrow at ten and he will give you a job.'

She looked down. The business card announced the name and address of a public course about twenty miles away in bold green lettering. It would mean a longer journey, but she would take anything.

'Thank you.' It seemed a very inadequate response when this stranger was giving her a lifeline, but she was thrown off balance by this unexpected offer.

'It's only temporary,' he told her briskly, 'but it's yours if you want it.'

With that he walked away. No smile, no small talk, just business, but she was so grateful. Perhaps things were going to be all right, after all.

'Wow!' Dave whistled. 'Who was that?'

'The man in the business suit.' Then she really laughed for the first time in days, more from relief than anything else, and she waved the card at her assistant. 'He's just given me a job!'

\*     \*     \*

She arrived half an hour before her appointment and spent the time having a look around. The place was very busy and the public had to queue for a game, but as far as she could judge, the course was in good condition, the practice field adequate, and the Pro's shop rather chaotic. Everyone was friendly and she became so involved in chatting to people that she had to run to make her appointment on time.

'Ah, Miss Palmer. Thank you for coming. I'm Jack Reynolds.' He shook her hand. 'Please sit down.'

She liked him instantly. He was about thirty, medium height, and with an open face, which she could see immediately was no stranger to a good laugh.

'Did Adam tell you about the job?'

'Adam?'

'Challoner.' His mouth twitched at her obvious confusion.

So that was his name. 'No, he strode in, gave me your card and told me to come and see you today.'

Jack laughed. 'Been his usual talkative self again, I see.'

His laughter was infectious and she grinned. 'I don't even know who he is.'

'Ah, well, I expect you'll find out eventually. Now about the job ...' He changed the subject so quickly that it was clear he wasn't going to enlighten her about the identity of her mystery man. 'We are in a bit of a spot,' he told her, 'we've engaged a professional, but he can't start for three months, and I expect you've seen how busy we are.'

She nodded.

'Would you consider helping us out until he's free to join us? We are quite desperate.' He smiled, holding her gaze steadily.

They couldn't possibly be as desperate as she was. 'Yes, I'd like that.'

'Excellent! Adam said you were an exceptional player and teacher.'

Her eyebrows rose in surprise. 'How would he know, he told us he knew nothing about the game?'

'Believe me, he knows perfection when he sees it.'

She was rather nonplussed by this remark, but was too excited about the prospect of her new job to give it much thought.

'Aren't you going to ask me about the salary?'

'As long as you're going to pay me something,' she remarked airily, 'I'll be happy to take the job.'

'I think we are going to get along fine,' he said as he stood up. 'Come and meet everyone and I'll explain as we walk.'

Two hours later she drove home feeling elated. She hadn't expected much in the way of money, but it really wasn't too bad, and it was a friendly place. It could be fun for a while, and although the job was only for three months, it would give her time to look for something permanent. She sent out a silent prayer of gratitude to her unknown benefactor.

'Kate!' Jack held up the phone. 'It's for you.'

She threaded her way through the

crowded shop. 'Is it my father?' she asked anxiously.

'No!' There was a look of absolute glee on his face. 'Oh, I like this. I never thought I'd see the day.'

'What are you on about?' She took the phone from his hand and marvelled that after only one week, she felt as if she'd been here forever.

Jack laughed and propped himself against the counter, waiting.

Giving him a playful shove, she turned her back. 'Hello?'

As soon as he spoke, she knew who it was; his deep voice was unmistakable.

'How's the job going?' he asked briskly.

'Fine. Thank you very much for recommending me.'

'Jack needed someone and you were out of work,' he stated simply.

'You did us both a favour, then.' Was he checking up on her? 'What can I do for you, Mr Challoner?'

Jack chuckled in the background and she turned her head to give him a warning look.

'Have dinner with me tonight.'

'Pardon?' That request - no, *order* - had taken her by surprise.

'I'm not in the habit of repeating myself,' came the sharp reply.

Of course he wasn't! 'I'm afraid that isn't possible.'

'Tomorrow, then.'

'Not any evening, Mr Challoner.' She was getting uneasy now. Was he looking for payment for getting her this job? 'I appreciate what you've done for me ...'

The muttered word was quite audible and she was surprised the phone didn't melt in her hand.

'I'm not seeking gratitude, Miss Palmer, I simply want us to share a meal. Nothing more.'

By now Jack was leaning over her shoulder trying to hear the other side of the conversation. She slapped him away and he laughed out loud.

'Is Jack bothering you?'

'Er, he's here, yes.'

'Tell him … No, let me speak to him.'

She did as ordered, and watched while Jack listened for a few moments, roared with laughter, then shook his head ruefully and handed the phone back to her.

'Hello.'

'If you won't have dinner with me-'

'Not *won't*, Mr Challoner, the word is *can't*.' She hadn't been out on a date for five years and she wasn't at all sure she wanted to spend time with this overpowering man.

He sighed. 'Make it lunch, then. You do get a break, I take it?'

'Yes, of course.'

'Good. I'll collect you at twelve tomorrow.'

She was left listening to the dialling

tone. 'But I haven't said I'd come,' she exclaimed in amazement.

'Kate, the word "No" isn't in Adam's vocabulary.'

'You know him well, do you?'

'We met at university and we've been friends ever since.'

'That's hard to believe. You seem to be complete opposites.'

'Don't be fooled by that brisk businessman image. He is human, I can assure you, though I've never known him to chase a woman before; it's usually the other way round.'

'He's not chasing me!' She was alarmed at the suggestion, unable to admit, even to herself, that the force of his personality had already quite overwhelmed her.

Jack chuckled again. She'd been right about him; laughter did come easily.

'If you were friends from university, how come you are managing a public golf course, and he …' she waved a hand in the air, 'he's whatever he is?'

'I don't manage this place, Kate, I own it.'

'Oh, I'm sorry.' She apologised hastily. 'I didn't realise.'

'Easy mistake to make.' He didn't sound at all offended. 'Adam and I started out in business together, but I'd always dreamed of owning my own golf course, and when this became available I bought it, got married and settled down.'

'You've made a great success of it,' she complimented.

'Yes, it's a good life and I'm content, but Adam is a high-flyer and work is what he lives for.' He gave her a thoughtful look. 'Why won't you go out with him this evening?'

'I can't, I have a disabled brother. Dad looks after him during the day and works at night, and I do the other shift.'

'Oh, I'm sorry, Kate. That doesn't leave you much time for a life of your own. What's wrong with him?'

'Hit-and-run driver left him paralysed.'

'Oh, God, that's terrible.'

She clenched her hands as the familiar fury surged through her. 'Paul was only fifteen and a brilliant golfer with a good career ahead of him, but one callous man brought that all to an end. If I ever come across him, I'll tear him apart with my bare hands.'

'Would you like to bring your brother here one day?' Jack suggested kindly.

'Thanks, but I think it would break his heart if he saw the course and couldn't play.'

She was nervous about the prospect of lunch with Adam Challoner. She knew enough about him to guess that he'd stroll in dead on the stroke of twelve and not give her a chance to refuse. Although she'd met him only briefly, she could see he was a man you didn't argue with.

Her hair needed a trim, she noted as she ran a comb through it, but luxuries like that were inclined to be put off, as were new clothes. Still, her dark grey tailored trousers were smart enough and she'd brought along a clean blouse to change into, the pale green highlighted her delicate colouring and almost matched her eyes. She viewed herself in the mirror, put on a little lipstick, the only makeup she ever wore, and decided that she would have to do. She just hoped he didn't take her anywhere too elegant.

The minute hand clicked onto the hour and the door opened right on cue. He strode in, making her heart beat uncomfortably. What on earth was she doing even contemplating going out with a man like him? Not, of course, that she'd been given any choice in the matter.

'Ready?' Expectantly, he held the

door open for her.

She only had time to grab her purse before he was ushering her to his car. 'What's the rush?' she complained.

'How long have you got for lunch?' he asked.

'An hour and a half.'

'Then we haven't any time to waste, have we?' He waited while she fastened her seat belt, then drove out of the gates.

It was only then she looked at him properly, and was relieved to see that he was wearing casual clothes - chocolate brown chinos and a cream open neck shirt, but the cut and style of them screamed money.

Realising that she was in danger of making a fool of herself, she stared out of the window, as the gold course slipped by. 'Where are we going?' she asked.

'There's a pub by the river where the food is excellent.' He cast her a quick glance. 'Are you hungry?'

'I'm always hungry.' She grinned. 'It takes a lot of energy teaching people to play golf.'

'I expect it does.' His gaze swept over her briefly and then back to the road ahead. 'You look as if you could do with a good meal.'

'Thanks!' she replied indignantly, 'I've always been slim and nothing changes that.' Then she saw his lips twitch with amusement. Wow! He almost smiled, she thought, as her own generous mouth curled into a grin and she relaxed. It was comforting to know he had a sense of humour, though of course, as a friend of Jack's it made sense.

When they reached the pub, he led her through the bar and into the garden at the back.

'Oh, this is lovely,' she exclaimed. 'It's right on the river.'

'As it's such a nice day, I thought you

would like to eat out here.' He chose a table under a large oak tree, and held a chair out for her.

When they were settled, she looked around and sighed happily. 'This is perfect.'

'Yes, it is,' he remarked softly, his eyes never leaving her face.

She felt herself flush under his gaze and reached for the menu to hide her discomfort. Golf had been her whole life, she'd had very little time for boyfriends and she'd certainly never had to deal with a mature man like this. He had the most probing way of looking at her and it was unsettling. She was quite out of her depth and wasn't sure if she was afraid or excited.

'What are you going to have?' he asked.

'Mineral water, please …' She chewed her bottom lip thoughtfully, 'and steak and kidney pie.'

When he ordered the same for himself,

she couldn't help asking, 'Don't you drink, either?'

'I like a drink, but never when I'm driving.'

His reply could have been from a script. He was making himself more and more attractive. The hit and run driver had probably been drunk, and that was why he hadn't stopped to help her brother.

'I wish everyone else felt the same,' she told him with feeling.

'You sound as if you've had experience of irresponsible drivers.'

'I have.' She then found herself telling him about Paul and he listened with a frown of concern on his face. His gentle questioning had her talking freely, telling him far more than she would normally have revealed.

'That driver didn't only ruin one life, did he?' His long fingers curled over her hand in sympathy. 'Is that why you refused to have dinner with me?'

She nodded and explained about the arrangement she had with her father.

'Can't you employ a nurse to help so that you can have some time to yourself?'

'Do you know how much that costs?' she asked.

'I'm afraid I don't.'

'Well, I'll tell you. Too much!'

At that moment their lunch arrived and he skilfully changed the subject, making her laugh as he related some of the escapades he and Jack had got up to in their youth. This was quite a different man from the one she'd met in Gordon's office. It seemed that there were two sides to his character that he could change as easily as flipping a coin. Kate settled back in her chair, becoming more and more at ease in his company.

'What were you doing at Chiverton Oaks?' she asked, her curiosity getting the better of her.

'I was there for a meeting and to have a look around.'

There was a pause but he didn't elaborate, and she didn't like to pry any further. When they'd finished eating, he looked at his watch, stood up and held out his hand. 'Come on, let's walk.'

She slipped her hand into his as if it was the most natural thing to do. 'Have I got time?'

'Yes. I'll deal with Jack if you're late back.'

'I have a lesson at two.' She looked up at him anxiously.

'I'll get you back in time.' He smiled at her. 'Don't worry.'

How wonderful to hear someone tell her that. The last five years had been nothing but worry, and she longed to lean on this strong man beside her.

'Tell me about your golfing career,' he asked, as they continued their walk.

She was so at ease in his company by now that she chattered away about the short time she'd been on the circuit and how much she'd loved it. When she reached the part where she'd had to come home and leave her dreams behind, she stopped talking and rubbed the back of her neck. 'I'm getting a crick in my neck looking up at you all the time. How tall are you?' she wanted to know.

'Around six feet five. How tall are you?'

'Five feet five.' She spied a fallen tree and dragged him over to it. 'Sit on that,' she ordered.

He did, then reached out and pulled her towards him, smiling. 'Is that better?'

Her face was now level with his and she wasn't sure if it was better or not. He wouldn't kiss her in broad daylight, would he? She soon got the answer when he leant forward and touched her mouth with his. It was only a brief butterfly type of kiss, and she had the overwhelming desire to wrap her arms around his neck and kiss him back. Alarmed by her reaction to him she stepped away and he released her at once. 'I must be getting back. I've already lost one job, I don't want to jeopardise this one as well,' she joked, giving herself time to pull herself together. There wasn't room in her life for romance and it was no good her thinking anything could come of this. She would only be laying herself open to more disappointments.

She raced into the shop five minutes late, and found Jack holding out a bucket of balls for her.

'Thanks.' Grabbing it she hurtled towards the door. 'Sorry I'm late.'

'Kate!'

She skidded to a halt and turned,

thinking she was going to be reprimanded, but Jack was grinning.

'I just wanted to know if you enjoyed yourself?'

'Er, yes, I did.'

'Turned the charm on, did he?'

That made her laugh. 'I don't think he knows how to, but I did see the flip-side of Adam Challoner, and I liked it.' Without waiting to hear Jack's comments about that, she headed for the practice ground as fast as her legs would carry her.

The next few days passed in a dream, they were so busy that she hardly had time to think about anything else, which was just as well, she thought wryly, because Adam had disappeared. Of course, she didn't really expect him to ask her out again, she told herself, because once he'd seen what an inexperienced girl she was, that would have been the end of his interest. She could see him with a glamorous, worldly woman on his arm, not someone like her.

She listened to the thunder, watched the rain coming down in torrents, and sighed. The bad weather had put a stop to her lessons. A drop of rain never put her pupils off, but it was never wise to be out there in a bad storm.

'Cheer up, Kate.' Jack handed her a cup of tea. 'It's going to stop this afternoon.'

'You sure?'

'Positive.'

'Does *anything* upset you?' she asked. She'd never seen him in anything but a good humour.

'Not much,' he admitted. 'I've got a wife and little boy I love dearly, and my golf course, which is doing well, so I don't reckon I have a lot to be unhappy about.'

He was a very fortunate man, she realised, and thought briefly about her own shattered dreams, but pushed them aside. Self-pity was something she tried never to indulge in. She and her father had been able to keep Paul at home and make his life bearable, and she considered it an achievement to be proud of.

'Jack, have you ever thought about building a driving range here? You've got the space for one and it would bring in a lot more business.'

He shoved his hands in his pockets and peered through the window. 'I've got plans to put one the other side of the café on that piece of spare ground. All I'm waiting for is Adam to come up with the money.'

'And will he?'

'Of course. I'll have it built by the end of the year.'

'Just what does he do?' she couldn't help asking.

'Well, I suppose you would call him an entrepreneur. He's got a phenomenal mind for business and is very successful at anything he gets involved in.'

Entrepreneur didn't tell her much. 'What does he specialise in?'

He grinned at her. 'His interests are varied, but generally it's anything that will make money and keep him busy. He's back, by the way.'

'I didn't know he'd been away. Has he been sunning him self on a tropical beach somewhere?'

That remark produced a chuckle. 'He wouldn't know how to relax. Ah, we were just talking about you.'

Kate spun towards the door in time to see Adam shaking the rain from his thick hair. He smoothed it back in place and scowled. 'Filthy weather.'

'Nice to see you, as well,' Jack chided. 'If you're in a lousy mood you can go straight out again.'

'I'm as docile as a lamb today,' he protested.

'Thank heavens for that.'

Kate listened to the banter between these two friends and looked from one to the other in amusement. They might be complete opposites but their fondness for each other was apparent.

'We're expecting you for dinner tonight,' Jack reminded him, then looked pointedly at Kate. 'You can bring a friend with you, if you like.'

'Kate?' Adam raised a dark eyebrow in query. 'Joan's a marvellous cook.'

How she wanted to say yes, but it was impossible. 'I would have loved to, but I can't.

'Then I won't be bringing anyone, Jack.' He smiled at Kate. 'Get your coat. At least you can have lunch with me, and we can go for a drive after. You can't be very busy in this weather.'

'But it's going to clear up and I've got a lesson in half an hour.'

'Who told you it was going to stop raining today?'

'Jack.'

'Don't take any notice of him; he sees the world through rose-coloured glasses. Trust me, it'll pour all day.'

'And he sees the world through cynical eyes,' Jack groaned.

'Not cynical, realistic,' Adam corrected him. 'I'm taking Kate out, am I going to have any trouble with you about that?'

Jack raised his hand in surrender. 'Would I dare?'

'But what about the lessons if it does stop?' Kate asked anxiously.

'I'll take them myself,' Jack told her. 'You go and enjoy yourself.'

'Er … are you qualified?'

'Do you mind?' He gave her a look of mock hurt. 'You are talking to the amateur champion of Oxford University.'

'I do beg your pardon!' She giggled at his expression. 'I've never seen you play.'

'That's easily put right. We'll have a

round early tomorrow and Adam can join us.'

'But he can't play.'

Jack lowered his head to whisper in her ear. 'He's telling fibs - plays off a two handicap.'

'Do you?' She asked in surprise.

He nodded, looking highly amused.

'Then why did you say you didn't know anything about the game?'

'It wasn't something I wanted anyone at Chiverton Oaks to know.

'What on earth were you being so secretive about?' she demanded. She never had found out why he had been loitering on the course, but how glad she was that he'd seen her.

Adam chuckled, a deep sound that seemed to resonate around the shop. He glanced at Kate. 'You coming?'

Of course she was. Every time she saw Adam Challoner, she fell deeper under his charismatic spell.

The next day, before the course had opened to the public, the three of them were poised on the first tee and Kate could hardly contain her excitement.

'Ladies first,' Jack said.

'No fear. I want to see what I'm up against.'

Adam took a driver out of his bag and had a practice swing. 'I think we should have a wager.'

'How much?' Jack asked.

'Not money.'

Kate breathed a sigh of relief. There was no way she could bet money on a game of golf. She watched Adam swing again and was impressed.

'Are you going to give me a handicap?'

They both looked at her in horror. 'Not likely,' Jack protested. 'I've seen you play.'

'Cowards,' she taunted.

'Too right!' Jack turned to Adam. 'What's it to be, then?'

Adam rubbed his chin thoughtfully.

'If Kate wins I'll buy her a new set of clubs and you can give her a bag.

'Done!' Jack agreed immediately.

'If you beat me, I'll see you get your driving range immediately.'

'But …?' She tried to protest but they ignored her.

'What do you want if you beat me?' Jack asked, rubbing his hands in glee about the driving range.

'A lifetime ticket to play your course whenever I want to.'

As they shook hands to seal the bargain, Kate stepped forward. 'Just a minute, haven't you forgotten something?'

They looked at each other, then back to her and shook their heads in mock bewilderment.

'Suppose you both thrash me, *I* can't compete with those kind of wagers.'

'Can't you?' Adam was doing a good job of pretending to be surprised.

He winked at his friend. 'What can Kate give us when she loses?'

She thumped his arm. 'Not so much of the "when".'

They stepped away from her, bowed their heads together and made a great play of whispering loudly with their hands half-concealing their mouths. She started to laugh. They were like a couple of schoolboys and it made her wonder, not for the first time, if men ever really grew up.

There was so much chuckling and banter that she decided to put a stop to it or she wouldn't be in any fit state to play. She was light-headed with laughter. Pulling them apart, she dragged them back onto the tee.

'If I lose I'll buy you both fish and chips in the club café,' she decided for them. 'I think half my wager is already paid - just for having to listen to you two carry on like you do!'

'But I get my food free in there,' Jack

protested.

'Good, that will make it less expensive.' She stood with her hands on her hips. 'That's my best offer.'

'Sounds good to me,' Adam said.

Jack nodded and took a coin out of his pocket. 'Let's toss to see who has the honour.'

'Oh, for heavens sake!' Kate took the driver out of Jack's bag and thrust it into his hands. 'You first, Adam next and me last.'

'Is she always as bossy as this?' Adam wanted to know.

'Nah. We've caught her on a bad day. I expect she's afraid we're going to beat her.'

'Well, if you don't stop messing about, I'll never find out if there's any danger of that, will I?'

The next couple of hours were the most fun she'd had in a very long time. They were both excellent players and she couldn't match them for power and distance, but her short game just had the edge on theirs. Her skill around the greens had always been the strong point of her game. Much to her delight, she beat them, but only by sinking a monster putt on the last hole. And if she had a sneaking feeling that they had bungled their last shots on purpose, she didn't let it bother her. To have matched them over eighteen holes was victory enough for her. She hadn't lost her touch; she was still an excellent golfer.

\*        \*        \*

The weeks were flying by and Kate couldn't remember when she'd been so happy. Adam regularly whisked her off to lunch, always to a different place. Once he'd taken her to his home, a beautiful Georgian house set in its own grounds, where they'd enjoyed a light lunch served by his housekeeper. The only blot on her happiness was the temporary nature of her contract. Time was running out and she would soon have to leave her job. How she wished she could stay.

Picking up her prize, she smiled with pleasure. They were the most beautiful golf clubs she had ever handled. Jack and Adam had insisted that they honour the wager and all her protests had been ignored.

'Adam's on his way over,' Jack announced as he burst into the shop.

Her face lit up with a radiant smile, her feelings open for anyone to see.

A rare frown appeared on his face. He looked her up and down, his eyes full of concern.

'You mustn't worry about me, Jack,' Kate said brightly. 'I haven't been this happy since my brother's accident but I'm no stranger to disappointment. I know it's unlikely Adam will want to keep on seeing me, and in a few short weeks I'm going to have to leave here.' She replaced the club she'd been holding into its smart leather bag and blinked rapidly to clear the moisture from her eyes. Then she turned back to Jack, her customary smile firmly in place. 'And that is going to be a terrible wrench.'

'And for us, Kate. I only wish we'd found you before we'd employed someone else.'

'Well, keep me on your list, and if you ever need anyone, whistle and I'll come running.'

'Try running to me,' said a deep voice from the doorway.

She looked up and laughed. It was only the customers in the shop who stopped her throwing herself into his outstretched arms, which was probably a good thing. She was well aware that she was almost certainly piling up heartache for herself by falling for this man, but she was determined to enjoy this stolen chance at happiness.

They dined at the pub he'd taken her to on their first lunch date, but he seemed preoccupied. She assumed he was in the middle of a business deal and left him to enjoy his meal without being distracted by a constant stream of chatter from her.

'Let's walk,' he said, when they'd finished their coffee.

He didn't keep to the river, but led her towards a country lane, away from the crowds enjoying the warm summer day. She glanced at him apprehensively a couple of times; his silence was making her heart thud in fear. He was holding her hand tightly, but was this the end? Was he bracing himself to tell her that he wouldn't be seeing her again? She steeled herself for the blow, determined that he would see her smile as he walked out of her life.

When they found a quiet spot, he leaned against a tree and pulled her into his arms.

It was *not* a goodbye kiss!

Finally, he broke the heated embrace

and cupped her face in his hands. 'This isn't enough, Kate,' he told her huskily. 'I want more; I want to be able to take you to the theatre, restaurants, dancing; I want privacy to hold you, touch you… I want to *love* you.'

'Love?' she whispered, hardly daring to breath.

He kissed her again, only tenderly this time. 'Yes, I love you, my beautiful girl. I've loved you from the moment I saw you on that practice field.'

She hugged him and he folded her in a crushing embrace.

'Does this mean you feel the same?'

'Oh, yes, I love you so much.'

He held her away so he could look into her eyes, and became the businessman for a moment. 'You must let me help you, Kate. I can arrange for you to have nurses to look after your brother.'

'I don't know that Dad would allow it.'

'Let me meet him,' he urged. 'It isn't right that you should both carry this burden when I'm in a position to do something about it.'

She hesitated, knowing her father would not accept help from someone who was a stranger to him.

'Marry me, Kate.'

'You want to marry me?' she gasped.

'Of course, what do you think this is all about? I want you for my wife and I am quite desperate.' He kissed the end of her nose and smiled. 'And your father could hardly refuse help from his prospective son-in-law, could he?'

'No, he couldn't.' Suddenly her world was full of hope. 'Can you come round before seven one evening?'

'Tonight. And you haven't said if you'll marry me, yet.'

'Yes! Oh yes, of course I will,' she declared. 'And tonight would be fine. I'll cook dinner for you.'

*     *     *

'I'll get it, Dad.' Kate's feet hardly touched the floor as she hurried to see Adam again.

'Hello, my darling.' He kissed her firmly. 'Is everything all right?'

'Yes, wonderful. Dad and Paul are looking forward to meeting you.' She took hold of his hand and led him into the lounge.

'This is Adam,' she introduced proudly.

Her father smiled and was about to shake hands with him when there was a cry of anguish from her brother. He dropped his hand and rushed to his son's side, but she just stood clutching Adam's hand as she viewed the scene in disbelief. Her brother had gripped the arms of his wheelchair and was trying to pull himself upright, but it was the look of hatred on his face which stunned her, for he was looking straight at Adam.

'Call the police,' he cried. 'That's him. That's the brute who left me to die!'

She held onto Adam because she wasn't sure she could stand on her own. 'You've made a mistake, Paul.'

'No, I haven't. Do you think I could ever forget that face as he looked down at me with those cold, unfeeling blue eyes?' He lifted an accusing finger. 'Still got that flashy bronze Jag, have you?'

She felt Adam rock back as if he'd received a physical blow, and she looked up at him imploringly. 'Tell him he's wrong.'

When his gaze met hers, she gasped at the bleakness in his eyes, and her world of happiness shattered into tiny fragments.

'Kate!' her father shouted. 'Get him out of here and call the doctor.'

She ignored the request, her whole

attention focused on the silent man beside her. 'Defend yourself, please!'

But he didn't utter a word as he released her fingers from his arm and left.

'Oh, my God!' she moaned. 'It can't be true.' But his silence had already condemned him.

'Kate! Pull yourself together and call the doctor.'

She must have gone through the motions, though she couldn't remember having done so, but the room was soon full of people. Doctor, paramedics and the police stood silently, watchfully, occasionally jotting a few notes onto their small notepads. Her father and brother did all the talking; she was too shocked to string a coherent sentence together.

After the ambulance had left for the hospital, and the police had gone, she slumped into a chair and buried her head in her hands, rocking back and forth in despair. The pain of losing Adam was so bad she couldn't even cry.

Relieved to be alone for a while, she rewound the scene in her mind. There was one detail she knew she would never forget, a detail that had imprinted itself upon her numbed brain. Her brother had nearly managed to stand up as the fury had ripped through him. He was so certain that Adam had run him down … The fact penetrated her shocked senses.

But it couldn't have been - *it couldn't*!

But it didn't didn't matter how vehemently she declared his innocence; the absence of a denial condemned him utterly. And there was his reaction when Paul mentioned the car. Every nuance of expression had screamed his guilt.

'Kate, I'm sorry, sweetheart.'

She jumped as her father put his arm around her shoulder. She had been so lost in misery that she hadn't heard him return from the hospital. It was hard to concentrate; hard to think of anything but the bleakness in Adam's eyes as he'd walked away.

'How's Paul?' she managed to ask.

'He's going to be all right! Did you see him trying to stand?'

She nodded.

'The doctors reckon that the shock has kicked his system into life, and they are hopeful that he will now make a full recovery.'

'At least something good has come out of this terrible night,' she murmured.

'Are you going to be OK?' her father asked with concern.

She shook her head slowly.

'I don't know, Dad. I keep thinking this must be a nightmare and I'm going to wake up in a minute,' she gulped, 'but I'm not, am I?' She looked at her father in utter disbelief. 'Adam *couldn't* have been that driver.'

'Paul hasn't any doubt about it.'

Kate sprang to her feet and started to pace the room.

'I can understand you defending the man you love,' her father said gently, 'but face the facts, Kate. You don't know much about him, do you? And the way he reacted makes me believe Paul is right, and he is the man we've been looking for this past five years.'

She shook her head in frantic denial. 'That's just the point - it was five years ago; Paul was badly injured and his memory might not be as clear as he thinks it is.'

Her father stood in front of her and took hold of her hands. 'If there has been a mistake - and I hope there has been for your sake - then the police will soon sort it out.'

'But the damage will have been done. There will never be a chance for us ...' She couldn't go on, for she knew that any happiness with Adam had vanished the moment her brother had accused him.

'Do you remember the photo-fit the police made after the accident?'

She nodded.

'Well you have to admit that it looks uncannily like him.'

'Oh, come on Dad! That sketch is so bad it could be any of a hundred men.'

'Your love for Adam is clouding your judgement.' Her father sounded cold, removed.

'And what if Paul's hatred is clouding his?' Her composure was beginning to crumble. 'Dad? What if …?'

'Why don't you go to bed,' her father urged. 'You're distraught.'

Her laugh was devoid of humour. 'Don't you think I have *reason* to be distraught?'

He sighed. 'I wish I could ease your distress, but I don't know how. And to be truthful, Kate, I can't be anything but happy that my son is going to recover at last. Whether Adam Challoner is guilty or not, he has done us a great favour tonight.'

'Oh, I'm sure that will be a comfort to him,' she said scathingly.

'Why don't you go to the hospital?' Her father changed the subject. 'Paul wants to see you and we are not restricted to visiting times.'

'No! I won't see him until it has been proved without a shadow of a doubt that Adam was the driver.'

'That isn't fair, Kate,' he reprimanded.

'I'm sorry, Dad, but you must give me time to come to terms with this.' Blinded by sudden tears, she stumbled from the room to seek the solitude of her bedroom.

She went into work as usual the next day; there didn't seem to be anything else to do. Her father was at the

Hospital and she was far too on edge to stay in the house on her own.

'I didn't expect you today.' Jack's eyes were like hers, smudged from lack of sleep.

'You *know*?' she asked, her voice trembling.

'Yes, Adam phoned me last night from the police station.'

Kate clutched the edge of the counter as the shop began to spin violently. 'They *arrested* him?'

'No, he went thereof his own accord.' He ran a hand over his eyes. 'He didn't do it, Kate.'

'Of course he didn't!' Thankfully the room had steadied, but she still held on for support. 'But why didn't he say so when he was with us? Why did he just walk away and leave everyone believing he was guilty?'

'Even you, Kate?' Jack asked softly.

'No, no! The evidence was damning, but I can't accept that he would act in such a callous way.'

Jack nodded with satisfaction. 'I'm glad you feel like that.'

'I want to see him,' she implored. 'Is he at home?'

'No, the police are holding him. They've got to check something before they can release him. *If* they release him.'

She caught hold of his arm. 'What do you mean - *if*? All he's got to do is prove it wasn't him and that's the end of it, surely?'

'It isn't as easy as that-'

'Jack! You're frightening me. What is going on?'

'I can't tell you, but he's got his reasons for acting the way he is.'

'Reasons?' Now she was getting angry. 'He is being accused of a terrible crime, one which could lead to a lengthy jail sentence, and you say he has his *reasons*.'

She started towards the door, but Jack

caught hold of her. 'Where are you going?'

'To the police station.'

'He doesn't want to see you, Kate.'

Her anger drained away to be replaced by a terrible numbness, a dull, leaden feeling of rejection.

'Of course he doesn't, I forgot for a moment; any feelings he had for me must have been destroyed last night.'

The rest of the day was a blur. Kate gave lessons and served in the shop, but she was running on autopilot, too numb to feel, to do anything but the most basic of tasks, and for that she was grateful, because if she let herself think, she would fall apart.

It was just before closing time when her father walked into the shop and by the expression on his face, she knew something had happened.

She took a deep breath. 'Tell me!'

'They've released him. He's

innocent.'

She cried properly for the first time, and tears of relief began to trickle down her face.

'Thank God!  So Paul was wrong, it isn't anything to do with Adam.'

'Not exactly.'  He found her a chair but she refused to sit down.

'What do you mean?'

Her father evaded the question, looking clearly uncomfortable. 'Paul recognised him because he is the image of the man who ran him down. It was an understandable mistake.'

The word *mistake* echoed through her thoughts. A mistake had shattered both hers and Adam's lives. 'You haven't answered my question,' she demanded.

'The man who injured Paul was Adam's younger brother.'  Her father broke the news as gently as possible.

She groped blindly for the chair and sat down before she collapsed as the implications of his revelation tore through her. It was someone in his family, *his brother*, and she knew that Adam would carry the guilt as if it were his own. She had doggedly clung to the hope that things would turn out all right for them, but the gap between them was becoming insurmountable. 'So they've now arrested his brother?'

'No, Kate. His brother died in a motorway pileup two days after Paul's accident, and the Jag was a write-off, that's why the police never found it.'

She was afraid to ask, but she had to. 'And did Adam know what his brother had done?'

'No!' Jack strode into the shop. 'He'd been in America for a month, and only returned for his brother's funeral.'

She looked at her father and he nodded. 'The police have checked.'

'Adam had no idea,' Jack told her. 'It was only when the car was mentioned that he realised Paul was talking about his brother. There wasn't another Jag in that colour, it had been a special order - a one-off.'

Jack put the kettle on to make tea for them. 'The boys were hard to tell apart, and although Ricky was four years younger, they were almost identical in looks, but their characters were completely different. Adam was always the steady, honest and reliable type, Ricky was reckless and didn't give a damn for anyone else.'

Kate wrapped her fingers around the mug, which had been thrust, into her hands. She was so cold. The more she heard of this story, the more miserable she felt.

Her father took her hand and patted it, bringing her back to the present.

'Will you go and see Paul, sweetheart? He's nearly out of his mind with worry about you.'

When she walked into the ward, Paul held out his hands and she grasped them. Even through her distress she couldn't help feeling a leap of joy to see him moving his arms so freely.

'You're looking wonderful,' she told him.

'That's more than you are.' His green eyes, so like hers, clouded with concern. 'I'm so sorry, Sis. You're the kindest person in the whole world and I've ruined everything for you.'

She couldn't allow him to carry this guilt. 'You mustn't feel like that. You believed you saw the man who'd left you in the road after the accident, and you reacted as anyone would have done.'

'I've written to him,' he blurted out, 'and told him that we don't hold him responsible for his brother's actions, and he mustn't blame you for what happened. He loves you, Kate, he'll come back, you'll see.'

But she knew he wouldn't. He would feel guilty because it had been one of his family who had caused them five years of grief. No, he wouldn't return to her; it was finished.

'Kate?' Paul's voice broke through her thoughts. 'I'm learning to walk again and the doctors say there is no reason why I shouldn't regain full mobility in time. I'll be able to play golf again.'

This was something they'd dreamed about, and pushing her own unhappiness aside, she smiled. 'You owe me a game as soon as you're on your feet.'

His face lit up with pleasure. 'Yes, and I'll play in some amateur competitions until I'm good enough, then I'll try for my Players' Card.' He hesitated. 'I *was* good, wasn't I?'

'You were terrific, and you're only twenty now so you're still young enough to start over.'

'So are you, Sis. I'm going to be all right now, so you're free and it's time you put yourself first. Twenty four is not too old to start playing the circuit again.'

Free? Yes, that was true, she was free of the need to look after Paul, free of Adam. She swallowed past the lump in her throat. One was the cause of joy, the other of indescribable anguish.

Kate's last day at Jack's course had arrived and she wasn't sorry. There were too many memories here

'What are you going to do?' Jack wanted to know.

She shrugged, not caring what tomorrow brought. There was only one person occupying her thoughts. 'How's Adam?'

'He's managing to function by throwing himself into one deal after another.'

'He sent a lovely reply to Paul's letter …' She tailed off and straightened some boxes on the shelf in front of her.

'I wrote to him as well, but he didn't answer.'

'If Adam has got one glaring fault, it's too much pride, Kate.' He gave her a sympathetic look. 'I told him that you had never doubted his innocence, and I think he believed me but it's hard to tell at the moment. He seems to have locked his emotions up and thrown away the key.'

'Damn his pride!' Kate swung the bag of clubs onto her shoulder - not the ones Adam had bought her, because she couldn't touch them without crying - but her old set. 'I've got one more lesson to give, then I'm finished here.'

She didn't know what made her look round, but she knew he was there. It was a replay of the first time she'd seen him, even the suit and tie were the same, but he'd clearly lost weight and his brilliant eyes were dull from lack of sleep.

'Keep practising,' she told her pupil,

'I'll be back in a minute.'

Her hopes rose as she hurried to where he was standing, but her smile vanished when he stepped back, keeping her at arms length. 'Adam,' she whispered, but he didn't even greet her.

He thrust a document into her hand. 'This is for you. I own Chiverton Oaks now and that's a contract for your old job back.' Then he turned and strode away.

At the end of the day, she said a sombre farewell to Jack and the other staff, and drove home, relieved she didn't have to go back there again with all its memories.

'What are you going to do?' her father asked later that evening, and not for the first time.'

She wished everyone would stop asking her that, she thought irritably.

'Are you going back to Chiverton Oaks?'

'No!' Suddenly the apathy that had

been clouding her thoughts cleared, showing her exactly what she must do. She grabbed the contract and left the house at a run.

*       *       *

When Adam opened the door, she stepped inside before he had time to react.

'We've got to talk.'

He ran his hand through his hair. 'There's nothing to say.'

'Oh, yes there is!' She slapped the contract into his hand. 'You can keep that, I don't want it.'

He frowned. 'What are you going to do, then?'

'Don't you start!' she exploded. 'I'm sick and tired of being asked that question.'

'Kate, you were unfairly dismissed and it's right you should have your job back.'

'Oh? And you think that by reinstating me, you've done right by me?'

'No,' he turned the contract over and over in his hands, then said sadly, 'it would take a lifetime to do that.'

'Then take a lifetime.'

Adam looked startled, and she felt like stamping her foot in exasperation. 'I've had enough of this nonsense. I'm not going to let you throw away what we had. I love you too much to do that.'

His head shot up and he searched her face earnestly.

'Why do you look so surprised?' she demanded. 'Did you think I would change my mind?'

'Yes,' he said quietly.

'Oh, you blasted idiot.' Tears were streaming down her face now. 'I don't want the Pro's job, I want *you*.'

Grinning broadly and looking years younger than he had when she walked in, he stepped forward, sweeping her off her feet and into his arms. 'Oh, God! Kate, I thought I was going to have to spend the rest of my life without you.'

'We are not going to spend one more minute apart.' She wrapped her arms around his neck. 'I love you Adam, and if a disaster like this hasn't destroyed our love, then nothing ever will. Whether you like it or not, I'm yours.'

'I *like*.'

Then he headed for the stairs, like a boisterous schoolboy, taking them two at a time.

## THE END

**If you enjoyed this Barley Book Handbag Romance, why not try some other titles in the series:**

Better the Devil ... by Andrea Presneill
I.S.B.N.: 1902691105

A Christmas Crisis by Beryl Mattews
1902691121

Manhattan Magic by Laura Hart
I.S.B.N.:1902691024

Love Restored by Lindy Benton
I.S.B.N.:1902691016

An Echo in Time by Kate O'Neill
I.S.B.N.:1902691105

The Gold-diggers by Charlotte Brooke
I.S.B.N.:1902691164

The books are available in your local bookstore and also from:

**www.barleybooks.co.uk,**
or direct from:

**Barley Books**
**P.O. Box 103**
**Leeds LS169YD**